This edition published by Parragon Books Ltd in 2014 and distributed by

Parragon Inc.
440 Park Avenue South, 13th Floor
New York, NY 10016
www.parragon.com

Based on the book *The Hundred and One Dalmatians* by Dodie Smith, published by The Viking Press.

ISBN 978-1-4723-4152-5

Printed in China

Read the story, then turn over the book
to read another story!

Bath · New York · Cologne · Melbourne · Delhi
Hong Kong · Shenzhen · Singapore · Amsterdam

Roger Radcliffe was a musician.
He lived in a little house in London
with Pongo, his pet Dalmatian.
One day, Roger got married.
His lovely new wife was named
Anita—and she had a lady
Dalmatian named Perdita.
Soon, Perdita was expecting her first
litter of puppies. Life seemed perfect
until one day, an old friend of Anita's,
Cruella De Vil, came to visit.

"Where are the puppies?" Cruella demanded.

"They're not expected for another three weeks," Anita replied.

"You must let me know when they arrive. I just adore Dalmatian puppies—their coats are so beautiful." And with that, Cruella swept out of the house in a flurry.

Three weeks later, Perdita and Pongo became the proud parents of 15 puppies. Roger, Anita, and Nanny, the housekeeper, were delighted.

But the very next day, Cruella returned. "Fifteen puppies!" she cried, excitedly. "I'll buy all of them."

"Oh no, you won't," said Roger. "They're not for sale."

"You fools! You'll be sorry!" Cruella cried, storming out of the house.

One night soon after, while Roger and Anita were out for their evening walk, two men came to the door.

"We're here to inspect the wiring and the switches," said the tall one.

"Electric company," said the short one.

"You're not coming in here," Nanny told them, guessing that they were up to no good. She was right, because the men were Cruella's henchmen, Horace and Jasper Badun!

Horace and Jasper pushed past Nanny. She tried her best to stop them, but they locked her in a room upstairs. By the time Nanny escaped, the men were gone—and so were the puppies!

The police immediately launched an investigation, but the puppies were not found. In the end, Pongo said to Perdita, "We'll have to find the puppies ourselves."

Pongo decided to try the Twilight Bark. This was the quickest way for dogs to send and receive news across the country.

That evening, when the two Dalmatians were taken for their walk, Pongo barked the alert—three loud barks and a howl—from the top of Primrose Hill.

After a moment an answering bark was heard. "It's the Great Dane at Hampstead!" Pongo said to Perdita, and he barked out his message.

Before too long, the Twilight Bark reached an old sheepdog named Colonel, who lived on a farm in the countryside.

Colonel's friends—a horse named Captain and a cat named Sargent Tibs—listened too. They were all shocked to hear that 15 puppies had been stolen!

"That's funny," Tibs said. "I heard puppies barking over at the old De Vil house last night."

"But no one lives there now," said Colonel. "We must go and see what's going on."

So, Colonel and Tibs went quietly up to the old De Vil house and peered through a broken window. Inside the house, the Baduns were relaxing in front of the television. All around the room there were puppies.

Not 15—but 99 of them!

Colonel quickly returned
to Captain's stable and
loudly barked the good
news. Within no time at
all, the Twilight Bark sent
the message all the way
back to Perdita and Pongo.

The two Dalmatians set off
across the snowy countryside as fast
as they could to rescue their puppies.

Meanwhile, Cruella was checking up on Horace and Jasper. "I want the job done tonight!" she shouted.

Then the trio discussed her plan to use the puppies to make fur coats!

Sargent Tibs was hidden away listening, and he could hardly believe his ears. He knew there wasn't a moment to lose— he had to save those puppies!

Once Cruella had left, Horace and Jasper went back to watching their television show. Tibs took the moment to help the puppies sneak away.

"Faster!" he hissed.

All 99 puppies made it out of
the room. Then Tibs led them very
quickly down the stairs. He could
hear the two men following them!

Sargent Tibs told the puppies to hide under the stairs.

"Shh. Here they come," whispered Tibs, hoping they wouldn't be discovered.

"Double-crossin' little twerps," said Jasper. "Pullin' a snitch on us."

"It ain't fair," said Horace.

While Tibs did his best to protect the puppies, Perdita and
Pongo met up with the Colonel outside the De Vil house.
"Our puppies, are they all right?" asked Perdita.
"No time to explain," said the Colonel. "There's trouble."
Hearing that, Perdita and Pongo ran to a window and
crashed right through. The puppies started
to flee, while their parents stopped
Horace and Jasper in their tracks!

Leaving the Baduns in a heap on the floor, Perdita and Pongo found their puppies a safe distance away in the Colonel's barn.

"Everybody here? All 15?" Pongo asked.

"Your 15 and a few more," replied Captain. "There are 99!"

Perdita and Pongo didn't want to leave any of the puppies for Cruella to find.

"We'll just have to take them all back to London with us," said Perdita. "I'm sure Roger and Anita will look after them."

Perdita, Pongo and the puppies set off back to
London, leaving a trail of paw prints in the snow.
But as they were crossing an icy road, Pongo heard
the honking of a car horn. "Hurry, kids!" he cried.

Sure enough, it was Cruella De Vil! She was
following closely behind them. The Dalmatians
ran faster and made it to a village where
a friendly Labrador was waiting.

The Labrador had arranged a ride home for the
Dalmatians in the back of a van. But Cruella and the
Baduns were waiting outside! How would they sneak past?
Luckily, Pongo stumbled upon the perfect solution!
"Come on, kids! Roll in the soot!" Pongo said.
They were all going to look like Labradors!

And that is how the Dalmatians snuck right past
Cruella and the Baduns. The van was only a short
distance away.

But, as the last of the puppies hurried into the van,
a clump of snow fell on one of them. Cruella was now
watching closely. She noticed the clean puppy!

"There they go!" she shouted, as the van pulled away.

Cruella raced after the van and
tried her best to force it off the road!

"Hey, lady, what in thunder are
you trying to do?" the driver shouted.
But he managed to stay on track.

Cruella was not so fortunate.
She ended up in a ditch,
along with the Baduns!

Safe at last, and back home in London, Roger wiped Pongo's face clean. "Pongo, boy, is that you?" he said.

"And Perdy," said Anita, "oh, my darling."

Nanny quickly brushed the soot from the puppies. "They're all here, the little dears!" she exclaimed. "And look . . . there's a whole lot more!"

"A hundred and one," said Anita. "What will we do with them?"

"We'll buy a big place in the country," said Roger. "We'll have a Dalmatian plantation!"

And that's exactly what they did.

The End

Now turn over the book
for another classic Disney tale!

Now turn over the book
for another classic Disney tale!

The next Christmas Eve, Jock and Trusty came by to see Lady, Tramp—and their four new puppies!

"They've got their mother's eyes," said Trusty.

"There's a bit of their father in them, too," said Jock, watching a mischievous little gray puppy.

Everyone was happy that Tramp had become part of the family.

The End

Jock and Trusty ran after the wagon. They barked loudly
to scare the horses, and the wagon crashed. Tramp escaped!
    Meanwhile, Jim Dear and Darling had arrived home.
Lady lifted the curtain to show that Tramp had caught
the rat and saved the baby. Jim Dear was very grateful.
He immediately rushed to find Tramp and bring him home.

CITY
POUND

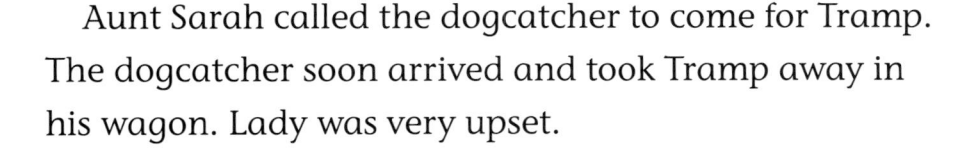

Aunt Sarah called the dogcatcher to come for Tramp.
The dogcatcher soon arrived and took Tramp away in
his wagon. Lady was very upset.

But Aunt Sarah was not happy. The baby's crying had woken her up, and she had found Lady and Tramp in his room. She thought they were hurting the baby.

Meanwhile, Lady was barking with all her might and pulling on the heavy chain. At last, the chain broke free from the doghouse. Lady ran inside to help Tramp.

Tramp had chased the rat under the baby's crib and accidentally knocked it over, making the baby cry. But Lady was happy because the baby was safe— Tramp had finally caught the rat.

Just then, Lady spotted a rat creeping into the
baby's room! She couldn't chase it because of the chain.
She could only bark.

"Stop that!" Aunt Sarah called. "Hush."

But Tramp heard, and rushed back to Lady. "What is it?"
he asked.

"A rat in the baby's room," Lady replied.

Tramp ran into the house and saw the rat. He had to catch
that rat before it hurt the baby!

Tramp tried to explain. "I thought you were right behind me, honest," he said.

"Good-bye," Lady replied. "And take this with you." She returned the bone that Tramp had given her, and turned her back on him. Tramp walked sadly away.

Before long, Tramp arrived. He had brought
a juicy bone for Lady. But Lady was angry with
him. She thought Tramp had only looked out
for himself and had let her get caught.

Back at home, Aunt Sarah chained Lady to the doghouse in the backyard!

Lady was so sad, even Jock and Trusty could not cheer her up.

Poor Lady had been caught by the dogcatcher
and taken to the dog pound!

Luckily, the dogcatcher soon came and read
her collar. He knew where to take her.

"You're too nice a girl to be in this place," he said.

Lady and Tramp ran away as fast as they could. When Tramp thought they were far enough away, he turned to check on Lady. But she wasn't there!

The next morning, on the way home, Lady and Tramp passed a chicken coop.

"Ever chased chickens?" Tramp asked. He couldn't resist.

Lady did not like the idea, but she followed him anyway. She discovered it was quite fun to do something adventurous! The chickens ran around the yard squawking and squealing.

Suddenly, Lady and Tramp heard an angry voice.

"Hey, what's going on in there?" the farmer called.

Tramp and Lady
accidentally picked up the
same piece of spaghetti.
The next thing they knew,
they were kissing!

Once they'd finished eating, the happy
pair walked to the top of a hill and gazed up at the full moon
that shone over their town. It was a beautiful night. Lady and
Tramp were falling in love.

Then Tramp took Lady to have supper at Tony's
Restaurant. Tramp's friend, Tony, liked Lady and fed
the pair his specialty—spaghetti with meatballs!
He served it to them at a candlelit table, and played
a romantic song as they ate.

"It's off!" Lady said with relief.

The beaver was happy too. He could use the muzzle as a handy-dandy log puller. Lady and Tramp thanked the beaver and left the zoo together.

The apes, the alligator, and the hyena were no help at all. Then Lady and Tramp found the beaver. He loved to chew, and soon bit right through the muzzle strap!

"Oh, poor kid," said Tramp, looking at Lady's muzzle. "We've gotta get this thing off. Come on."

Tramp took Lady to the zoo—maybe one of the animals could help her.

Lady ran and ran. Soon some big, mean dogs
started to chase her. Lady was scared, and ran
into an alley. Luckily, Tramp heard all the
barking and raced to Lady's rescue.

Aunt Sarah took Lady straight to the pet store.
"I want a good, strong muzzle," Aunt Sarah said.
The muzzle scared Lady. She jumped off the
counter and ran out the door, not knowing where
she was going.

Her two cats were not very nice, either. They made a mess of the house and pretended that Lady had caused the trouble.

"Oh, that wicked animal!" said Aunt Sarah.

Not long after the baby was born, Jim Dear and Darling decided to take a trip. Aunt Sarah came to take care of the baby. Her two Siamese cats came, too. Aunt Sarah was not very nice to Lady.

Tramp was another dog who was sometimes in the neighborhood. He didn't have a warm home and family. He liked to wander the streets, looking for scraps and helping his friends escape the dogcatcher.

One day, Tramp overheard Lady saying that Jim Dear and Darling were expecting a baby.

"What's a baby?" Lady asked.

"A home wrecker, that's what," said Tramp.

Lady wasn't sure what Tramp meant, but she had a feeling that her happy life was about to change . . .

Lady lived very happily with her owners, Darling and Jim Dear. When Lady grew up, they gave her a collar with a name tag. Lady proudly showed her collar to her friends, Jock and Trusty.

"She's a full-grown lady," said Jock.

Lady and the TRAMP

Read the story, then turn over the book
to read another story!

Bath · New York · Cologne · Melbourne · Delhi
Hong Kong · Shenzhen · Singapore · Amsterdam

This edition published by Parragon Books Ltd in 2014 and distributed by

Parragon Inc.
440 Park Avenue South, 13th Floor
New York, NY 10016
www.parragon.com

ISBN 978-1-4723-4152-5

Printed in China